Part of the team . . .

Kin Travis had brought the catch-can with him to pit road so he could practice with it. The first time Waddy pulled in, Kin waited until just the right moment, then he casually stepped over the wall as if he'd done it a thousand times. Junior noticed, grinned, and gave him a quick thumbs-up before continuing with his own work.

Kin slid the catch-can onto the overflow pipe and held it there for about twenty seconds, trying to imagine what it would be like on race day with cars coming in and out of the pits and the rest of the crew running around.

He pulled the can free, stepped back, and immediately turned to climb over the wall, swinging one leg high, scooting his rear end across the wall, and sliding onto the other side.

This time Tach noticed Kin's work. The mechanic smiled and nodded. "That's the way, kid," he murmured with a wink. "That's how we all got here. Practice, practice, practice."

Collect all the
NASCAR Pole Position Adventures:

* coming soon

HAMMER DOWN

POLE POSITION ADVENTURES NO. 5

T.B. Calhoun

HarperEntertainment
A Division of HarperCollinsPublishers

HarperEntertainment

A Division of HarperCollins*Publishers*
10 East 53rd Street, New York, NY 10022-5299

This is a work of fiction. The characters, incidents, and dialogues
are products of the author's imagination, or if real, are used ficti-
tiously. Any resemblance to actual events or persons, living or
dead, is entirely coincidental.

First printing: April 1999

Cover illustration by Tony Randazzo
Designed by Susan Sanguilly

Printed in the United States of America

ISBN 0–06–105965–X

98 99 00 01 02 10 9 8 7 6 5 4 3 2 1

CONTENTS

- - - - - - - - - - - - - -

EARLY BIRDS

Kin Travis rolled over on his side and glanced at the alarm clock again: 5:00 A.M. He groaned. *So much for all those alarms*, he thought. Kin had been lying in his narrow bunk, wide awake, for more than an hour. He sat up, running one hand over his eyes and another through his short brown hair. Yawning, he swung his legs over the side of the bunk, hit the OFF button on the alarm clock, and stood, being as quiet as he could. He didn't want to wake up his seven-year-old brother, who was huddled under the sheets in the little bunk over the RV's front section, or their grandfather, who was snoring lightly in the reclined driver's seat.

Kin padded to the RV's tiny bathroom, smothering another yawn. He had set three alarms to make sure he was up by 5:15—the clock radio, his own watch, and the watch on Grandpa Hotshoe's wrist.

Kin didn't want to be late for work again, not after yesterday. He definitely didn't want to risk messing up now—not when things were going so well. Back in the days when he was living in California, following his grandfather's exploits on TV and in the newspapers, Kin never could have dreamed that he would have a job with a real NASCAR pit crew before he even turned sixteen. But it was true. Kin and his younger brother and sister had come South to spend the summer with their grandfather, Hotshoe Hunter, an ex-race car driver. Almost before Kin knew it, Hotshoe's friend Waddy Peytona had offered him a job.

Yesterday had been Kin's first day. It hadn't started out very well. Kin had arrived at the garage at 7:30, only to find that the entire crew was already there—crew chief Cope, head mechanic Tach, suspension man Carl, Waddy's sixteen-year-old son Junior, and of course, Waddy himself. Waddy hadn't been pleased that his new crew member was late, which was why Kin wanted to be the first one in the garage this morning. The gate opened at six, and he planned to be there waiting, wearing his new uniform with his name on the chest.

When he came out of the bathroom, Kin saw his grandfather standing in front of the stove, lining the bottom of a skillet with bacon. Grandpa Hotshoe was wearing an old terrycloth robe, and his gray hair and beard looked more unkempt than ever. "Grub's on," Hotshoe said in a loud whisper. "Why don't you make some toast while I finish the bacon and eggs?"

"Deal." Kin's stomach was already rumbling at the delicious smell of the sizzling bacon. He grabbed a loaf of bread and glanced up at his younger brother as he ripped it open. "Should we wake Laptop?"

"Let the kid sleep," Hotshoe whispered back. "I think he had a big day yesterday, playing with Laura and those kids they met." He grinned. "As I was going to bed last night, I heard him mumbling in his sleep. Something about a million dollars, and buried treasure . . . "

Kin shook his head and grinned back. His brother Larry, better known as Laptop because of the portable computer he carried everywhere, wasn't exactly a typical seven-year-old kid. He was a computer genius with a wild imagination and little patience for anyone who wasn't as smart as he was.

"By the way, Kin," Hotshoe said, only a little louder than the bacon's sizzle. "I'm really sorry I didn't get you up in time yesterday morning. I just never thought. . . "

Kin popped a couple of slices of bread into the toaster and smiled at his grandfather. "That's all right, Grandpa," he said. "It's my job—my responsibility. I'll make it up to Waddy today. I'll be the first one there."

Kin left the RV at 5:40. Glancing around, he couldn't help smiling at the scene around him. Seabreeze Raceway's infield was already packed with vehicles of every shape and size—RVs like Grandpa Hotshoe's, camper vans, station wagons with tents pitched nearby, even an old converted school bus or two. Hotshoe's friend Infield Annie's big silver Airstream trailer was parked in the spot next to the RV, with a striped awning connecting the two vehicles. Kin saw a light shining through the curtained window near the back of the Airstream. He guessed that Annie was already up, getting ready to head over to her portable restaurant and start cooking breakfast for hungry crew members, drivers, and fans. He wondered if his twelve-year-old sister, Laura, who slept in the Airstream, was up to help her. *Probably not*, he thought with a grin. *Lazy Laura's always hated getting up early. And now that she's practically a singing star, she probably needs her beauty sleep more than ever.*

It was still a little strange to think about Laura's newfound talent. From the moment she'd picked up their mother's old Wabash guitar, the songs had seemed to pour out of her—familiar old country tunes, the latest pop hits, anything people requested. Laura seemed to know them all.

It's almost like Mom is helping her somehow, helping her sing and play. Kin's smile faded as he thought about his parents. Even now, more than a year after World Wide Airlines Flight 888 had gone down, it still gave him a pang when he realized he would never see his mother or father again. He still couldn't quite believe they were gone.

But there was no time to think about that this

morning. Pushing all sad thoughts out of his mind, Kin headed for the road leading to the garage area.

When he reached it, he saw that the gate was still locked. There was no one around. Suddenly feeling foolish, like a geeky kid showing up early on the first day of school, Kin quickly turned away. Luckily, nobody was around to see him. Sticking his hands in his pockets, he wandered aimlessly down the length of the chain-link fence.

As he counted off the minutes, he wondered what the day would bring. Would Waddy let him help with the car today, or would he spend most of his time watching again? Would the crew be finished in time to go to the dance being held at the track tonight? If so, would Kin have the guts to ask Teresa Peytona, Waddy's smart, beautiful, sixteen-year-old daughter, to dance with him?

At ten minutes to six, Kin started back toward the long sliding gate at what he hoped looked like a normal pace.

In the short time he'd been gone, some twenty people had gathered at the gate. Kin walked up as casually as he could, trying to act as if this were old stuff to him. No one more than glanced at him.

When the gate opened, Kin started through with the others. The guard stopped him. "Hold up, there, son. Where's your pass?"

"I, uh . . ." Kin was embarrassed. All the planning and getting up early—and he'd forgotten his pass!

He spun around to run back to the RV. But he'd taken only a few steps when he saw his grandfather striding toward him, still dressed in his old bathrobe, waving the pass.

"Grandpa, you're a lifesaver," Kin said breathlessly as he grabbed the pass.

Hotshoe chuckled. "No problem. Run on, now. I know you want to get to work before anyone else gets there."

"Thanks again!" Kin turned and ran toward the gate.

A WAY TO THE TREASURE

When Laptop woke up, he found he had the RV to himself except for Scuffs, the little yellow dog that had adopted the Travis kids at the last race track they'd visited back in Tennessee. It had seemed only natural to bring him along with them to North Carolina. He already felt like part of the family.

"Hey, boy," Laptop greeted the dog. He hopped down from his bunk and reached up to retrieve his Apricot 07 portable computer from under his pillow. "I smell bacon. I guess that means Grandpa and Kin had breakfast without me. Typical."

Sometimes it bothered Laptop when the others forgot about him. At other times he didn't mind at all. Today was one of those other times. Laptop had big plans for today, plans he couldn't possibly put into action if his grandfather forced him to tag along with him.

Laptop smiled, picturing how happy Aunt Adrian would be if all went according to plan today. He could almost see it now—her clear gray eyes would light up, her stiff, angular shoulders would relax. . . . He still remembered how worried she had looked when he'd last seen her. He hated seeing her so unhappy.

Aunt Adrian ran an art gallery with her third husband, Smedley. That was just about all Laptop had known about her until his parents had died. Then he and Kin and Laura had gone to live with Aunt Adrian and Uncle Smedley in their big old house in Boston, where the heaters never quite seemed to burn off the constant chill in the cavernous rooms. At first the kids had thought their aunt was just as chilly as her house. But beneath her cool, proper exterior she was really a warm, caring person. She had done her best to be a good substitute parent to all of them. Uncle Smedley was another matter. . . .

Laptop suspected it had been Smedley's idea to send them to stay with Grandpa Hotshoe while he and Aunt Adrian spent the summer in Paris for an important art show. Luckily, the plan had turned out pretty well as far as Laptop was concerned—traveling around with Grandpa Hotshoe was interesting, to say the least. Things hadn't gone quite as well for Aunt Adrian. A couple of days earlier, she'd suddenly turned up in North Carolina, looking grim and flustered.

She hadn't told the kids the reason she was there. But she had told Grandpa Hotshoe, and Laptop and Kin had overheard. Smedley had stolen a valuable painting and sent back a ransom demand. Aunt Adrian had to come up with a million dollars in a week, or the painting would be destroyed. Aunt Adrian didn't want to tell the police—she didn't want Smedley to go to jail. In spite of what he'd done, she still loved him, though Laptop didn't quite understand why. Dull old Uncle Smedley had never seemed all that lovable to him.

Laptop walked over to the stove and peered at the frying pan, which was empty except for a layer of grease. "I hope they gave you a couple of pieces, at least," he told Scuffs.

"Worf," Scuffs barked. Suddenly the little dog's ears perked up, and he turned and ran toward the RV's door. "Worf!"

"Come in," Laptop yelled, hoping it was his sister. The day before, the two of them had made a promising start on their plan to help Aunt Adrian with her problem. And Laptop had something new and cool to show Laura this morning.

The thin metal door creaked open, and Laura poked her head in. Her hair was tied back in a loose ponytail, and her round blue eyes looked sleepy. "Hi," she greeted Laptop with a yawn. "Want to come over to Annie's with me and get some breakfast?"

"In a minute." Laptop flipped open the top of his Apricot 07 computer and hit the switch to bring it to life. "I want to show you something first."

Laura sighed as she bent down to give Scuffs a good-morning pat. When her little brother got that gleam in his eyes, it usually meant he was up to something. And when Laptop was up to something, there was no telling what could happen. "What is it?" she asked. "Don't tell me you figured out how to borrow a bulldozer to help us dig up whatever you think you found out there yesterday."

"Better." Laptop grinned. "Check it out." He waved one hand at the computer screen.

Laura leaned over his shoulder and peered at the words on the tiny screen. Laptop had pulled up a Web page that seemed to be some kind of advertisement. In big block letters, it read:

ZOBO TREASURE HUNTING SERVICE
LOW RATES—BASED IN N. CAROLINA
YOU FIND THE SPOT—WE DIG UP THE GOLD!

At the bottom, in smaller print, was an e-mail address.

"I found it last night when I was surfing around just before I went to sleep," Laptop explained, sounding excited. "It was weird—it just seemed to pop right out at me when I did a search! It's just what we need to save Aunt Adrian."

Laura frowned as she read over the ad again. The evening before, when Laptop had first described the way the metal detector he'd borrowed had gone crazy over a certain spot, she had been a little excited in spite of herself. But now, in the bright light of morning, she couldn't help feeling skeptical. What were the chances, really? How likely was it that there was some fabulous buried treasure out there in the big field behind the grandstand, and that Laptop had found it?

"Not so fast," she said. "We don't want to start calling in professional treasure hunters unless you're absolutely sure there's really a treasure."

Laptop shrugged and grabbed a piece of bread out of the package lying open on the counter. "I am sure," he said. "What else could it be? A metal detector doesn't lie." He stuffed the bread into his mouth.

"I know," Laura said, trying to be patient. Laptop might be a genius, but he was only seven. "And I know you want to help Aunt Adrian. So do I. But think about it—just because there's something metal down there, it isn't necessarily treasure. We have to be logical about this."

"Logical," Laptop repeated through a mouthful of half-chewed bread. But before his sister was out the door, he was typing in the e-mail address listed at the bottom of the ad.

THE GRAY GHOST

Kin hurried down the length of the long garage, hardly glancing at the cars parked inside. He felt like running, but he forced himself to keep to a fast walk. He didn't want to seem too eager.

But he did want to beat the others to the Peytona team area, not just so Waddy couldn't chew him out for being late again. He had another reason.

Ever since he was a kid back in California, hearing stories about Grandpa Hotshoe and watching NASCAR races on TV, Kin had dreamed of being in the driver's seat of a real race car someday. The day before, for a few minutes, he'd finally made that dream come true—sort of. Maybe sitting in Waddy's Ford in the empty garage, dreaming of what it would be like to hear the ignition catch and the engine roar around him, wasn't quite the same as really driving. But for now, it was the best he could do. If he hurried, he might have a few minutes to himself before the others arrived. . . .

Kin broke into a jog as he neared the Peytona area. He smiled when he saw that it was still empty. *Awesome!* he thought, his eyes turning to the Ford Taurus with Waddy's number, eighty-two, painted on the sides. He stepped forward and ran a hand over its roof, which felt cool and smooth.

"Awesome," he murmured out loud. He put his other hand on the edge of the paneless driver's side window and got ready to hoist himself through. But at that moment, a flash of movement from farther down the garage caught his eye. He turned and saw a cluster of men dressed in gray coveralls coming toward him.

Kin scowled, disappointed, and stepped away from the car. It was the Gray team, another pit crew. As usual, they were walking briskly in a group, looking neither right nor left. Kin doubted they even saw him standing there. Still, he knew that his driving daydreams would have to wait for another morning. With the Gray team working in the next stall, just steps away, he wasn't about to climb into the Ford and pretend to drive.

As the Gray team approached, Kin craned his neck, trying to catch a glimpse of the man in the middle of the tightly bunched group. He'd never gotten a good look at the Gray team's driver, though Junior Peytona had told him about them. He had explained that they'd appeared on the NASCAR scene recently, showing up at every race, dressed only in gray and speaking to no one unless they had to. They always qualified for the races— never placing first, never placing last, always running somewhere right in the middle. Nobody knew much else about them. Even their team sponsor was anonymous.

The gray-clad crew members stopped at the back of their gunmetal gray hauler. As soon as a crewman at the front of the group opened the doors, the man in the middle quickly climbed into the hauler's tunnel-like dimness. He wore a large, floppy-brimmed gray hat that hid his face, so Kin caught only a glimpse of him.

Kin frowned. Something about the way the driver walked had seemed familiar, though he wasn't sure why. Maybe he'd seen the man on TV, or maybe he just reminded him of someone else he knew. . . .

The other Gray team crew members followed the mystery man into the hauler. All except one.

He looked about Kin's age, and he came over and unlocked a tool chest only a few feet from where Kin was standing.

"Is his name really Gray?" Kin asked.

The boy in gray glanced back at the hauler. "We're not supposed to talk to anybody," he said.

Kin shrugged. "I'm not anybody," he said. "I won't tell."

"Well, then, yes, it's Gray. Mosby Gray."

"Mosby? That's a weird name."

"Oh yeah?" The boy glanced at Kin's name tag. "That so—Kin?"

Kin blushed. "It's short for McKinley," he explained quickly. "I'm named after William McKinley, some president from like a hundred years ago."

The other boy glanced nervously over his shoulder. "Well, he's named after a colonel in the Confederate Cavalry. John Singleton Mosby. He was sort of a Confederate Rambo on horseback. The Yankees called him the 'Gray Ghost.'"

"Cool." Kin glanced curiously at the gray hauler once again. Then he opened his mouth to ask the other boy his name—there was no name tag on his gray uniform. But before he could say another word, the boy grabbed a socket wrench out of the tool chest, turned, and hurried back toward his hauler.

Kin shrugged as he watched him go. "See you," he said, though the other boy was already too far away to hear.

CHARGING AHEAD

"That's four more biscuit-and-hams and one biscuit-and-sausage, Annie," Laura said, hurrying behind the counter of the portable tent that served as Infield Annie's homestyle restaurant.

Annie didn't bother to look up. She just nodded briskly, her broad, kind face flushed pink from the heat of the stove. Despite the early hour, the tent was crowded with customers. Most of the crew members and drivers were over at the garage by now, but there were plenty of hungry fans ready for a heaping helping of Annie's famous Southern cooking.

Laura glanced at the door just in time to see Laptop come running in, with Scuffs panting after him. She frowned, wondering what he'd been doing since she'd seen him back in the RV. If he'd gotten himself into trouble, she was sure to be blamed for it. *It's not fair,* she thought, wiping a bead of sweat off her forehead. *Why should I always be the one to keep track of him? Why can't Kin take a turn once in a while?*

Laptop's eyes were bright with excitement as he hurried toward the counter. After checking to make sure Annie wasn't close enough to overhear, he motioned for his sister to lean toward him. "The treasure hunters say they'll do it for a fourth of whatever we find," he whispered. "All we have to do is show them where to dig."

Laura gasped. "You—you mean you contacted them?" she sputtered. "After I told you not to? I thought you—"

"And they say they can be here this afternoon!" Laptop interrupted.

Laura's mind raced. She couldn't believe her little brother had actually been crazy enough to hire real treasure hunters. Actually, she could believe it—she should have known Laptop wouldn't be put off by a few calm, logical words from her. When he got his mind set on something, it stayed set.

"I also stopped by to tell Jane and Eddie,"

Laptop went on. "I thought they'd want to be there when the treasure came up. But they weren't around."

Jane Thompson and Eddie Harris were a couple of racing fans around Laura's age. Laura and Laptop had met them in the infield the day before. It was Jane's father's metal detector that had started Laptop's whole treasure-hunting scheme.

Laura chewed on her lower lip, slowly wiping down the counter with the rag she kept tucked in her apron pocket as she thought about what Laptop had just told her. She didn't want Annie to start wondering why she wasn't working and come over and interrupt them. Then she'd never get a chance to talk Laptop out of this.

Then again, should she really try to talk him out of it? True, it was a pretty crazy idea. But what if there was something valuable buried out there behind the track? Stranger things had happened. . . .

"I wish Aunt Adrian was here," Laura muttered. "Then we could just tell her about what you found and let her worry about digging it up—whatever it is."

Laptop stared at her in astonishment. "Are you nuts?" he exclaimed. "There's no way she'd ever believe us. Even Grandpa and Annie wouldn't believe us—you didn't tell them, did you?"

"No." Laura glanced over her shoulder to make sure Annie wasn't listening. "I didn't even tell Kin."

She didn't say so again, but she still wished their aunt was there. But Aunt Adrian was visiting a friend in South Carolina and wouldn't be back until sometime the next day.

Laura sighed. She still felt worried, but she decided to ignore the feeling. Sometimes it was easier just to sit back and let Laptop do what he wanted to do.

And you never know, she thought, tucking her rag back into her apron pocket. *If anyone could find some fabulous buried treasure at a race track, it would be Laptop!*

CATCH-CAN MAN

Kin was still staring at the Gray car when he spotted Waddy at the far end of the garage area, walking rapidly toward him.

Kin gulped, hoping that Waddy wouldn't be angry at him for just standing around when there was always so much work to be done. But when Waddy came closer, he saw that the stocky, dark-haired man didn't look mad at all. If anything, he looked embarrassed.

"I'm really sorry!" Waddy said, running one cal-lused hand over his close-cropped dark hair. "We blew it. When we stopped to grab some carry-out breakfast, Cope asked Carl what you wanted. Carl said he had no idea. I knew then that we'd left off a spark-plug wire—no one remembered to ask you what you wanted for breakfast. And what's worse, nobody remembered to tell you we were coming in late this morning." Waddy shrugged. "I left the others waiting for the food and came on ahead to, uh, apologize."

For a second, Kin was tempted to shake his finger at Waddy and lecture him on how important it was to be on time. But he decided Waddy might not get the joke.

"It's okay," he said instead. "No big deal."

Waddy nodded. "Before the others get here," he said, "what say we get started on teaching you how to be a catch-can man?"

Kin grinned eagerly. "That'd be great!" This time he didn't worry about seeming too eager. He couldn't wait to have a real job to do around the place, instead of just standing around feeling like a fifth wheel, trying to stay out of the others' way.

Waddy unlocked the hauler and pulled out the catch-can. It looked a little like an ordinary one-gallon lawn mower gas can, except that it was painted blue and yellow—Waddy's team colors—and it had a pour spout large enough to roll a tennis ball down. Also, its large, sturdy handle was on the side, not on top where a handle ordinarily might be.

Waddy held out the can for Kin to inspect. "This big spout is for letting gas in, not for pouring it out," he said. "This little short tube here is the vent, to let air out as gas comes in. You don't want to put your hand over it or block it off."

Kin nodded and followed as Waddy walked over to the back of the car.

"Look, listen, and learn, Kin," Waddy said, repeating one of his favorite sayings. "When the car comes into the pit—after it's passed you, so you don't get run over—you step over the wall and run up to the back of the car. Got that?"

"Yes, sir." The words slipped out before he could stop them, and for a second Kin felt embarrassed. All of Aunt Adrian and Uncle Smedley's lessons on manners must have rubbed off on him. But when he saw the pleased smile on Waddy's face, Kin felt better. *I guess Aunt Adrian's right*, he thought with a private grin. *I guess good manners really are welcome anywhere.*

He snapped back to attention, realizing that Waddy was speaking again. "Then you put the big metal spout of the catch-can over that short pipe sticking out of the back of the car," the driver said, pointing to the pipe in question. "See, it's about level with the fill tube on the side of the car. You with me so far?"

"Yes, sir."

"Now, the reason we need a catch-can is because gas is 'dumped' into the fill tube from an eleven-gallon can. There's no automatic shutoff like at a gas station pump. The gas man simply pushes the hose of the dump-can into the tube, the valve inside the hose opens, and the gas falls out of the can. Just like you'd turn a milk jug upside down and take the top off."

"Wow." Kin hadn't had any idea that was how it worked. The more time he spent at the track, the more he realized how much he had to learn.

"Now," Waddy went on, "if the first dump-can doesn't fill the fuel cell, which is usually the case on a pit stop, the gas man grabs a second one. That one will run over, and that's where you come in. The overflow is what the catch-can man catches in the catch-can. You got all that?"

"I think so," Kin said.

Waddy again pointed to the small aluminum pipe that stuck about two and a half inches out the back of the trunk. "When the car comes in, you and the gas man hop over the wall at the same time. He goes to the side of the car to start dumping the gas, and you head for the overflow pipe in the back. Don't jerk back when you feel the gas rush in."

"Okay." Kin thought he could handle that. "Then what?"

"When the car takes off, the gas in the fuel cell tries to flow out the overflow pipe. So keep the can against the back of the car as long as possible. You might even run a step or two with it."

Kin grinned. "Cool. Sounds kind of exciting."

"Catch-can man isn't the biggest job in racing," Waddy said, "but it's as important as any of them. Any time a dump-can is connected to the car, a catch-can man must be in place. Once the car takes off, you have two more things to worry about. Three, really. First, make sure you keep the hose pointed up. Don't spill what you've gone to so much trouble to catch. Second, keeping in mind the first, get back over pit wall as soon as possible. Pronto. Got that?"

"Yes, sir," said Kin.

"Third—and you have plenty of time for this—pour what's in the catch-can back into one of the gas cans so it can be weighed."

"Weighed?"

"Yep. When the gas cans are taken back to the pumps to be refilled, they're also weighed. That way we know how much gas we put in, which lets us figure our gas mileage. That way we know when to pit. It's hard to win a race when you're hauling five or six extra gallons you don't need. It's even harder if you're sitting over on the back straight-away out of gas."

"Right."

Waddy took a deep breath. "But do you know what this catch-can stuff is really all about?"

Kin hesitated, not sure what Waddy was driving at. "Um . . . "

"It's about safety." Waddy reached up and tapped Kin's forehead with one stubby forefinger. "Safety, safety, safety."

"Safety." Kin nodded. "Got it."

"The main part, the part that concerns me most"—Waddy jabbed his finger into Kin's chest—"is you. It's your safety I'm concerned about most. Your safety." He jabbed again. "If you haven't heard one word of what I've said this morning, you better hear these two, and I mean hear 'em good. Be careful. Be careful. Be careful."

Three jabs.

"First of all, as I said, make sure the car is past you before you step over the wall. The brakes could lock up, or I might have to swerve to miss something, and the car might slide into the wall. You don't want to be standing there if it does. And as you start over, look back down pit road and make sure no other car—especially the one in the next pit—is coming in too fast or sliding out of control. Got that?"

"Yes, sir."

"Done, then. And just in time." Waddy pointed at something over Kin's shoulder. "Here come the others with breakfast."

Kin turned quickly, wondering exactly who was included with the others. Was Teresa with them?

She wasn't, and Kin immediately felt embarrassed for thinking about a girl—even an amazing girl like Teresa—at a time like this. He had a lot to do and a lot to learn.

Besides, he'd see her soon enough. There was a big dance that night, and Kin planned to make sure he spent plenty of time with Teresa. He wondered what she would wear. . . .

"Hey, dreamer boy!" Tach called out. "You going to join us for breakfast or not?"

"Sure," Kin said quickly, feeling his face grow hot. "Sure thing. I'm starved." He hurried over to where the others were taking seats on the hauler's step bumper or on nearby toolboxes. He wasn't really hungry at all, not after the bacon and eggs Grandpa had made for him. But he sat down between Tach and Carl, who were arguing good-naturedly about who had ordered what, and reached for a cup of coffee. He liked being included with the group.

He especially liked it right at the moment. Right at the moment he wasn't being lectured to or fumbling for the right wrench or getting in anybody's way. In fact, at the moment, it seemed that he was as much a crew member as anybody. No one was ignoring him, but no one was paying him special attention either.

It made him feel like he belonged there.

TODAY WE HAVE TIME FOR LUNCH

Breakfast was leisurely. But as soon as the last bite of it had disappeared, the workday began in earnest.

The crew tinkered with the car all morning. When the track opened for practice at eleven, the work continued.

Three hard laps under the clock, then come in.

Check tire temperatures. Check shock travel. Talk.

Make a change or two. Back out.

Three more hard laps. In.

Compare times with before. Check tire temps, shock travel.

Talk. Make a change. Go back out.

Time and compare.

Kin had brought the catch-can with him to pit road so he could practice with it. The first time Waddy pulled in, Kin waited until just the right moment, then he casually stepped over the wall as if he'd done it a thousand times. Junior noticed, grinned, and gave him a quick thumbs-up before continuing with his own work. The adults didn't seem to notice what Kin was doing at all.

Kin slid the catch-can onto the overflow pipe and held it there for about twenty seconds, trying to imagine what it would be like on race day with cars coming in and out of the pits and the rest of the crew running around.

He pulled the can free, stepped back, and immediately turned to step back over the wall, swinging one leg high, scooting his rear end across the wall, and sliding off on the other side.

This time Tach was the only one who indicated he'd noticed Kin's work. The burly, gray-haired African-American mechanic smiled and nodded. "That's the way, kid," he murmured. "That's how we all got here. Practice, practice, practice."

The next time Waddy pulled in, Kin did a quick swing-leg-jump-slide over the wall and pushed the catch-can onto the overflow pipe again, this time with more force and certainty. But just as the hose hit the pipe, the car leapt forward. Kin went stumbling after the car, almost falling.

Cope caught him.

"I know you're supposed to chase the car to catch the overflow," the gangly, red-haired crew chief said. "But that's overdoin' it."

For the rest of the morning practice session, each time Waddy came in, Kin jump-slid over the wall and jammed the catch-can hose onto the overflow pipe as many times as he could. He could feel himself getting more and more confident.

The fourth or fifth time Waddy came in, Kin realized he was getting blisters on both his thumbs from pushing the handle of the can. Plus he was getting a raw tailbone from sliding over pit wall.

So he wasn't sorry when Waddy peeled away again and Cope said, "Those who want to can head on back to the garage. Waddy thinks this change'll do it. Looks like we're about ready for Happy Hour later today."

"What's Happy Hour?" Kin asked Junior, as they headed for the nearest opening in the chain-link fence.

— — — — — — — — — — — — — — — —

"It's the last hour of practice," Junior explained. "It comes after the cars that didn't qualify in the top twenty-five yesterday have finished their qualifying runs. Happy Hour is a shakedown run, a final try of what you think is your best race setup."

"And what if it doesn't work too well?"

"You change it if you can," Junior said. He shrugged. "Then you go home and don't sleep much."

A few minutes later, Waddy pulled his Ford Taurus into the garage and sat in the driver's seat talking to Cope. Then, as Waddy was climbing out of the car, Cope turned to the rest of the team, who were watching and waiting.

"Waddy thinks we're pretty close," Cope said. "But before we go changing anything, he wants an opinion from Kin."

The crew members all looked at Kin, then back at Waddy, clearly wondering what he was going to say.

Both feet now on the ground, Waddy pulled down on both pant legs of his driving suit, and wiggled slightly. "Kin," he said gravely, "do you think things are going well enough for us to take a break for lunch today?"

They all laughed, Waddy most of all. "Sure, boss," Kin said with a grin, recalling how hungry he'd been the day before when the crew had worked straight through the lunch hour. "I think that would be fine."

"You heard him." Waddy waved an arm at the crew and headed for the exit. "Let's eat!"

As the whole group headed for Infield Annie's restaurant, Kin walked with an extra spring in his step. After the hard morning's work, he felt even more like a real part of the crew than he had earlier.

THE REST OF THE PLAN

For Laptop, the morning had passed slowly. He'd wandered back and forth between the RV and Annie's restaurant so often that Laura had finally told him to go away and stop pestering her.

Laptop didn't really mind. Annie was starting to give him suspicious looks. The last thing he wanted was for any of the adults to guess what he was up to. They wouldn't understand—they'd probably be even more skeptical than Laura.

"They'll see, though," he whispered to Scuffs, checking his digital watch. "In just a few hours, they'll be able to see the treasure for themselves. And Aunt Adrian will be saved."

"Worf," Scuffs barked.

• • • • •

"Hey, Twerp Girl. Wake up. It's your big brother. Remember me?"

"Wish I didn't," Laura said tartly, glancing up at Kin, who had just walked into the restaurant with the rest of Waddy's crew. She couldn't help noticing how cool her older brother looked in his new team uniform, but she didn't say so.

"Hey, Mountain Laurel." Junior Peytona stepped forward to take his serving of beans and greens. "Are you going to sing at the dance tonight?"

Laura blushed. The older boy was staring at her with his frank, friendly brown eyes, and it made her feel a little nervous. "I don't think so," she said, pleased that he'd remembered her stage name. "But, um, I'm singing the national anthem at tomorrow's race."

Kin was glancing around the restaurant. "Hey, Laura, where's Laptop?"

Laura bit her lip. Why did Kin have to start wondering about their little brother today of all days? "Uh, I don't know," she said. "I—I guess he must be with Grandpa."

Kin shrugged, seeming satisfied with that. "Thanks, Annie," he said, accepting a heaping plate from Annie. With hardly a backward glance for Laura, he headed off to a table in the corner with his new friends from the pit crew.

Laura just hoped they'd finish and leave before Grandpa Hotshoe showed up—without Laptop. If they started to wonder where the little boy was, Laura was sure to end up in the middle of it.

When the lunch rush had trickled off to a few lingering customers, Annie glanced over at Laura, who was scrubbing out one of her big pans. "Why don't you take off, darlin'?" Annie said. "I can handle cleanup today. You ought to go have some fun—maybe rustle up those two kids you were telling me about. What were their names again?"

"Jane Thompson and Eddie Harris," Laura replied, setting the pan down on the counter.

Annie nodded thoughtfully. "Jane Thompson. I think I know her mama and daddy—big race fans. Follow the circuit for a week or two every summer." She nodded again. "They like my corn bread."

Laura smiled fondly at Annie, untying her apron. "Everyone likes your corn bread."

"Flattery will get you nowhere." Annie waved

her hands, but her broad face wore a big grin. "I already said you could go. So shoo, girl."

"Thanks, Annie." Glancing at her watch, Laura headed for the door. If she was lucky, maybe she had enough time to talk some sense into Laptop.

When she reached the RV, Laptop was waiting in the doorway, looking at his watch. "It's about time," he said. "I was just about to leave without you."

"Did you ever track down Eddie and Jane?"

Laptop shook his head. "Someone told me Jane's mom took them out shopping for the day or something." He shrugged. "So I guess it's just you, me, and Scuffs today."

"Oh." Laura wasn't very happy about that. At least with Jane and Eddie along, she would have had some chance of keeping Laptop under control. Still, there wasn't much she could do about that now. "All right. Then let's get going. I want to be back in plenty of time for that dance tonight."

THE TREASURE HUNTERS

When Laura and Laptop reached the big field behind the grandstand, Laura saw that it wasn't as empty as it had been when she'd seen it last. More and more people were arriving for tomorrow's race, parking their campers and trucks anywhere they could find a bare spot of ground.

"I hope no one parked a big old van on top of your treasure," she commented.

"Nope." Laptop pointed across the field. "It's way over there, almost in the trees. And it's in among a bunch of big rocks. Nobody will want to park there even if this place gets a lot more crowded."

"Hey, kids!"

Laura turned and saw a man and a woman standing in front of a black panel truck. They were both tall and thin, with curly black hair. The man also had a large, curly black mustache. Both adults were wearing large sunglasses and pin-striped gray coveralls. The man was waving at them. "Are you Larry and Laura Travis?"

"That's us!" Laptop answered eagerly, hurrying toward them. "Are you from Zobo Treasure Hunters?"

The man nodded briskly. "I'm Bo," he said. "This is my associate, Zo."

Laura wrinkled her nose slightly at the treasure hunters' odd names and even odder appearances, glancing at her brother worriedly. *Are these people for real?* she wondered. *Why did I let Laptop talk me into this ridiculous plan, anyway?*

Still, she couldn't really feel that worried. These people might give her the creeps, but they were professional treasure hunters. She'd seen their ad on the Internet herself. Besides, what could happen to them here in this field, with Seabreeze Raceway and hundreds of people only steps away?

Scuffs looked up at Bo, put his nose in the air, and sniffed. Then he let out a low, whimpering growl and backed up a few steps.

Zo laughed harshly. "Looks like your dog doesn't like us."

"He'll be okay," Laptop said. He picked up Scuffs. "He's not used to strangers, that's all."

"Enough chitchat," Bo said, sounding impatient. "Let's get moving. Hop in the truck, and we'll head to the site. You did say it's near here, didn't you?"

Laptop nodded. "Very near. I'll show you the way." He headed for the truck with his computer tucked under one arm and Scuffs under the other.

Laura glanced nervously at the truck. It had no markings at all on the outside. For some reason, Aunt Adrian's voice popped into her head: *Never accept a ride with someone you don't know.* It was one of a long list of safety rules she was always reciting to them. "Um, maybe we should walk over there," she said hesitantly. "It really isn't far. . . ."

"Don't be ridiculous." Bo gave her a chilly smile. "We need to drive our digging equipment over anyway. And there's no time to lose—not if you want your treasure today."

His logical words made Laura feel slightly foolish for worrying. "Oh," she said sheepishly. "Um, all right then." *After all, we're not in big-city Boston now,* she told herself. *And the sooner we finish this excursion, the sooner I can get back to the Airstream and decide what to wear to the dance tonight.*

Taking a deep breath, she followed her brother into the dark interior of the truck.

DANCING PARTNERS

Junior glanced at his watch. "Ten minutes to Happy Hour," he announced, just as an announcement came over the PA system saying the same thing. "Everybody ready?"

Kin set down the wrench he'd been cleaning and stretched out his back. Despite the fact that Waddy had claimed the car was ready to go earlier, they'd all been working nonstop since lunchtime— tweaking something here, making an adjustment there.

Cope, who was bending over the engine compartment of the blue and yellow Taurus, straightened up and used a clean shop rag to wipe the sweat from his brow. "Looks copacetic, boys. Button her up and push her out to pit road. I'm going to see if I can find Waddy a dancing partner."

Kin went over to help Junior lower the car's hood. As he pushed a chrome-plated clip through the eye of a pin—one of four that stuck up through the hood—he glanced at the other boy. "Dancing partner?" he asked uncertainly, images of Teresa passing through his mind. "Um, for Waddy?"

Junior grinned. "Don't worry," he told Kin. "Cope just wants to find Daddy a dancing partner for Happy Hour."

"Huh?" In Kin's opinion, Junior's explanation was as clear as fresh road tar.

"It's this way." Junior pushed up the rim of his baseball cap with one thumb. "In a race, cars run both side by side and nose to tail. What Cope wants to do is find someone to take turns with Daddy. First one or two laps in front, then one or two behind. That way, Daddy can find out how his car handles when there's someone right on his tail, and when he's tucked in tight against someone's rear bumper. The 'dancing partners' can come in, make some changes, and go out and try again—maybe with a different partner. Get it?"

Kin nodded. "Now I do."

Junior grinned. "Of course, Daddy'll probably do some real dancing at the shindig tonight if Mama has anything to say about it." He glanced at Kin. "What about you? You dance much?"

"I guess." Kin shrugged. "You know—school dances and stuff like that."

"Well, if you dance with a few different girls tonight, you'll probably find out each one dances a little different. Has her own style. Right?"

"Sure," Kin agreed. He didn't bother to tell Junior that he was planning on dancing with only one girl tonight. One special, beautiful girl with honey-blond hair and sparkling violet eyes. *If only I can work up the nerve to ask her,* he added to himself.

"Well, cars are the same way," Junior said. "Daddy needs to dance with a Ford, a Chevrolet, and a Pontiac. They have different aerodynamic characteristics and different effects on cars running behind them—and maybe even a little on cars in front of them. Daddy might find out, for example, that his Taurus is faster behind a Monte Carlo than behind a Grand Prix, but fastest of all when it's behind another Taurus—especially a really fast one like Rusty Wallace's."

At that very moment, as if on cue, Cope came running down pit road. "Okay!" he said. "Waddy's partner for the first waltz is Rusty Wallace. Let's get our Ford fired up and ready to go!"

A NEW CLUE?

Laptop glanced up from his Apricot 07 and sighed, shifting his weight on the jagged boulder he was using as a chair. Bo and Zo didn't seem to be making much progress in bringing up his treasure. After Laptop had guided them to the right spot, the pair had spent a few minutes unloading several pieces of equipment from the back of their truck, including a tiny lawn tractor with a digging attachment on the front. Laptop wasn't sure what to think—it was hardly the kind of heavy machinery he'd been expecting. Still, he guessed that Bo and Zo knew what they were doing. They were the professionals.

Laura, who was pacing nearby with Scuffs trotting at her heels, was looking more bored and annoyed with each passing minute. "Did you find anything yet?" she asked the treasure hunters for about the hundredth time.

Bo didn't bother to answer as he maneuvered the little tractor, but Zo shot Laura a venomous look. "We could work faster if you'd stop bugging us," she snapped.

"Well, I would stop bugging you if you'd hurry up," Laura shot back, crossing her arms over her chest and glaring at Zo.

Laptop cleared his throat. This wasn't looking good. How could Bo and Zo get anything done if they were wasting time arguing with Laura? "I'm sure they're working as fast as they can," he called to his sister. He glanced at Zo apologetically. "You'll have to excuse her," he said. "She's just worried about our aunt." On the ride over, he had told Bo and Zo all about Aunt Adrian's problem.

Zo didn't bother to answer. She just turned away to help Bo as the little tractor struggled to bring up another chunk of dirt.

Laptop peered at the digital clock in the corner of his computer screen. This was taking longer than he'd expected. He had already looked up the current exchange rate of gold and silver and the price of diamonds and several other precious stones on the open market. He wanted to be sure he knew what the treasure was worth when they found it.

If they ever found it.

"Worf!"

Laptop glanced over at Scuffs. The dog had stopped following Laura. Letting out another bark, he ran to a spot near the edge of the hole Bo and Zo had made and started digging, his little paws sending the dirt flying.

"Hey!" Bo cried, sounding annoyed as a small rock bounced off his tractor.

But Laptop hopped to his feet, almost dropping his computer in excitement. "I think he's trying to tell us something!" he cried. "He must think that spot is where the treasure is buried!"

Laura looked skeptical. "How would he know?"

But Zo looked almost as excited as Laptop felt. "Animals have a sixth sense about these things," she said, peering at Scuffs over the tops of her dark glasses. Laptop noticed that her narrowed gray eyes were glittering. "Let's give it a try."

Bo shrugged. "Whatever you say," he grumbled, shifting gears on the tractor and heading over to the spot where Scuffs was digging. "But get that creature out of my way unless you want him flattened."

Laptop hurried to grab Scuffs, hugging him tightly to his chest. He glanced over his shoulder at the race track stands. He couldn't wait to see everyone's faces when they heard about the treasure!

HAPPY HOUR IS OVER

When the red flag came out, signaling the end of Happy Hour and the closing of the track to further practice, Kin and the rest of the crew hurried back to the garage area. They watched anxiously as Waddy drove the Taurus into the garage and Cope went over to confer with him. They'd made several small changes during Happy Hour, but Cope hadn't said whether they'd helped or not.

"This is it," Junior muttered. "If the car's not right, we're up all night!"

Kin's heart sank as Cope came toward the crew, looking grim. Being part of the crew had its downside as well as its rewards. If there was a problem with the car, none of them would be going to that dance. And he would miss his chance to spend time with Teresa. . . .

After a second, though, Cope's freckled face broke into a wide grin. "Happy Hour really was Happy Hour for us today," he announced. "Waddy says the car feels great. So let's get things cleaned up here and get ready to have a good time at the Pit Road Scramble. The Seabreeze Eat, Greet, and Dance-Till-You're-Beat Frolic."

"It's 'Dance-to-a-Beat,' Cope," Junior corrected quickly.

"Doesn't matter to me," Cope said. "It's going to be fun, either way you say it!"

"I can't believe it!" Bo growled. "Don't tell me this is the treasure you kids have been blabbing about!" With a look of disdain on his narrow face, he held up a half-eaten old hot dog with one thumb and forefinger. Scuffs whined eagerly from Laptop's arms, struggling to get away and grab the hot dog.

Laura wrinkled her nose. "Ugh," she said. "I don't think so."

She was still having trouble believing she was here. The afternoon was waning, and she guessed that most people back at the track were already thinking about getting ready for the dance.

That's where I should be, too, she thought. Treasure or no treasure, this was taking an awfully long time. Besides, she couldn't quite shake the feeling that there was something—well, something not quite right about Bo and Zo. They still hadn't taken off their dark glasses, even though the shadows from the nearby trees were blocking most of the sun's rays by now.

Suddenly, with a loud "Worf," Scuffs finally broke free from Laptop's grip. The little dog launched himself at Bo, who was bending over to drop the hot dog. In one graceful move, Scuffs caught the hot dog in his tiny teeth—and knocked Bo's black mustache off with his stubby, wagging tail!

Laura stared, confused. "Wha—"

Laptop gasped. "You!" he shrieked. "It's you!"

"Who?" Laura demanded.

Bo stood up slowly, his thin lips stretching in an evil grin. "So you finally recognize me—us." He glanced over at Zo. She was grinning, too.

As Laura watched, the pair both reached up. With one swift move, Bo and Zo ripped off their curly black hair, revealing the sleek, matching silvery hair beneath. They removed the sunglasses, so the kids could see their matching silvery-gray eyes.

Now Laura recognized them, too. Her whole body went cold with terror. "You're those two!" she cried. "Those weird evil clones who kidnapped Laptop!"

She could hardly believe she hadn't seen it before. The narrow, crafty faces, the glittering, pale gray eyes. . .

A few days earlier the same pair had snatched Laptop while they were stealing classic cars from a race track in Tennessee. Laptop had barely escaped with his life.

"But I thought you were clones," Laptop said, hugging his computer to his chest. "Before, when you talked, you each said exactly the same thing at exactly the same time."

Bo laughed. "We're not really clones. We just pretended to be, to weird people out."

"We used the echo in the cave where we were keeping those cars," Zo added. She was grinning fiendishly. "Pretty cool, huh?"

Laura gulped. Glancing over at her brother, she saw that his face was paler than usual. She knew how he felt. She had read about insane people before, she'd seen them on TV and in the movies.

But now here she was, face-to-face with a couple of people who were obviously totally off their rockers. Bo and Zo weren't just criminals. They were crazy criminals.

Why did we trust these two? she asked herself helplessly. *I thought there was something strange about them from the beginning. And now . . .*

She glanced over her shoulder at the grandstand of Seabreeze Raceway. It looked very far away. So did the campers and vans parked at the other side of the field. She wondered if there was anyone in any of the campers right now, and if they could see what was going on here. But she doubted it.

When she looked at her little brother's frightened face again, she suddenly felt a tiny bit braver. Laptop was only seven, and he was counting on her. She turned to face Bo and Zo with her hands on her hips and tossed her head defiantly.

"What do you want from us?" she cried.

Bo reached into his pocket and pulled out a pistol. "That's for us to know and you to find out!"

PREPARING TO PARTY

Hotshoe came by just as the big rear doors of Waddy's hauler were closing. "Ready to let this boy go get ready for the dance, Waddy?" Hotshoe called to his friend.

Waddy grinned. "Anything for you, old buddy." He gave Kin's shoulder a squeeze. "Besides, young Kin here put in a good day's work today. He deserves a little fun tonight."

"Thanks, boss." Kin couldn't help feeling proud of himself. He had learned a lot that day—and more important, he had helped out the team. He couldn't wait to do the same on race day tomorrow. But first there was tonight's dance. . . .

Kin hadn't seen Teresa all day. He'd been too shy to ask Junior or Waddy where she was. He just hoped she was still planning on coming to the dance.

He also hoped his little brother and sister wouldn't hang around and embarrass him when he was trying to get to know her. Laura would probably keep herself busy with her own friends. But Laptop might be a problem—unless maybe Kin spoke to him. Came to an understanding. In other words, bribed him to keep out of his way.

"Where's Laptop?" he asked, trying to sound casual.

Grandpa Hotshoe was humming under his breath as he and Kin walked across the infield toward the RV. "Laptop?" Hotshoe shrugged. "With Laura, I expect."

Kin frowned. "I saw Laura at lunchtime. She said Laptop was with you."

"Are you sure?" Hotshoe furrowed his brow, looking a bit worried. "I haven't seen the boy all day. I just assumed—"

"Never mind," Kin interrupted, sorry he'd brought it up. If he knew Laptop, the kid had slipped away so he could play with his computer in peace. The last thing Kin wanted was to get caught up in some kind of search party, when he could be showering and changing for the dance. "You know Laptop. I'm sure he's fine."

Hotshoe nodded slowly. "You're probably right," he said, still sounding a bit worried.

TRAPPED BY THE TWINS

"I can't believe this," Laura muttered. "I really can't believe this is happening!" She pounded her fists against the interior of the black panel truck in frustration.

"Stop that for a second." Laptop was hunched over his Apricot 07. He just hoped its built-in cellular satellite phone wasn't thrown off by the truck walls surrounding them. He'd tapped them and discovered that they were some kind of extra-thick metal.

He shrugged. What other choice did they have? Laura certainly wasn't doing anything constructive to get them out of here. Ever since the evil twins had chased Scuffs away, herded them in here with that pistol, and locked the doors, she'd just been stomping around, tripping over the pieces of machinery still inside, and moaning and groaning about what they should have done. Laptop began punching in numbers.

"What are you doing?" Laura asked. "Who are you calling? Grandpa will be working, dummy, remember? Kin, too. It's a big practice day. And after they're finished, they'll probably go straight to that dance. They won't be sitting around in the RV waiting for a phone call from us."

"Maybe. Maybe not," Laptop replied calmly. "But Grandpa's got an answering machine, doesn't he?"

"Yeah," Laura said sarcastically. "An answering machine that he checks about once a month. He'll never get your message"—she gulped—"in time."

Laptop waved a hand for quiet as he heard the machine click on at the other end of the line. Then, speaking as clearly as he could, he said, "Grandpa, this is Laptop and Laura. We've been captured by the evil twins. They have us locked in a black truck on the far side of the field behind the grandstand. Please hurry. They're completely insane." He punched a button to hang up. "There," he told Laura with satisfaction. "That should do it."

Laura crossed her arms. Even in the dim light coming through the small, narrow windows high up in the truck's side walls, Laptop could see that she looked skeptical.

"All right, all right," he said. "Do you know Annie's number?"

"She doesn't have a phone," Laura said. "She always uses Grandpa's." Suddenly her face lit up and she started digging into her shorts pocket. "Wait a sec, though. Jane gave me her number the other day. I just hope I still—aha!" She pulled out a scrap of paper and handed it to Laptop.

He punched in the number. "I hope they're back from shopping," he said. He had to raise his voice a little to be heard over the sound of Bo's tractor, which had just roared back to life outside. "Uh-oh, I'm getting a machine. . . ." He cleared his throat and waited for the beep. "Hello, this is a message for Jane. Jane, this is Laptop and Laura. We're in big troub—"

"Hey!" An angry shout interrupted his words. Zo had just pulled open the truck's wide rear door. "What are you kids doing?" Brandishing a pistol, she jumped into the truck and grabbed Laptop's computer.

"Stop!" he cried, horrified. "Give that back!" He snatched at it, but Zo was already backing away, a sinister grin on her face.

"You won't be needing this," she cackled, snapping the laptop's lid shut. "I'd better just get rid of it for you." She turned and hurled the small computer as hard as she could out the door.

"No!" Laptop leaped forward, but Zo jumped out of the truck and slammed the door shut before he could reach her. He pounded against the metal with his fists. His computer—his precious Apricot 07, the last computer his father had ever designed— was gone. He was glad that at least Zo had closed it before throwing it out. Its tough, resilient case had probably protected it against the impact.

But that didn't make him feel much better. Without his computer, what chance did they have? Would he and Laura ever escape? Would he ever see his beloved Apricot 07 again? Would he ever see Grandpa again, or Aunt Adrian, or Kin, or Scuffs?

Laptop slumped down against the truck wall, feeling defeated. Why hadn't he sent a general e-mail alarm when he had the chance? Why had he wasted valuable time leaving phone messages that might not be found until Bo and Zo had . . .

He shivered. "What do you think they'll do to us after they find the treasure?" he asked Laura.

She shook her head. "Who knows?" she said grimly. "But whatever it is, I doubt we're going to like it."

THE PIT ROAD SCRAMBLE

"Hurry up, Grandpa," Kin said for the third time. "Your hair looks fine."

Kin was showered and changed and pacing back and forth in the tiny open space in front of the RV's door. He was itching to get over to pit road and find out what this dance was all about. He also wanted to see if Teresa was there yet—and ask her to dance before some other guy beat him to the punch.

"Hold your horses, boy." Grandpa Hotshoe gave his gray hair one last swipe with a comb. He glanced anxiously at the RV door. "Maybe we ought to wait for Laptop and Laura."

Kin groaned. "Come on, Grandpa!" he complained. "They're probably over there already, stuffing their faces."

"Okay, okay." Grandpa Hotshoe chuckled. "I

reckon you're probably right about that. I've never known either of those two to miss a meal if they could help it." He tossed his comb aside and winked. "All right, let's get over there before all the good-lookin' gals are spoken for."

Moments later the two of them were walking briskly toward pit road. When Kin saw the place, he could hardly believe the difference. From a drab strip of asphalt, pit road had become a bright swath of color and action. Each team was occupying the same pit it would use in the race. Every pit except one now contained tables and chairs decorated with team colors. The concrete wall behind the pits was festooned with banners.

In all that color, the grayness and emptiness of one pit stood out: the Gray Racing pit. Kin shook his head when he noticed it. *Don't those guys ever have any fun?* he wondered, thinking of the kid he'd talked to earlier.

But he didn't think about that for long. He was too busy taking in the sights. Along the grassy strip that separated pit road from the track were small tents and booths bearing the familiar names and logos of various fast-food chains and brands of soda and snack food.

In the middle of it all was a large tent flying a banner that read SEABREEZE CHAMBER OF COMMERCE. Thick, rich-smelling barbecue smoke coiled out from under the tent's raised flaps.

"Here's the drill," Hotshoe explained to Kin as they strolled along pit road. "The Seabreeze Frolic is in three parts. The first part is a picnic, just for us NASCAR folks and local officials and so forth."

Just then they came within sight of the Peytona pit. Kin grinned when he saw it. On the wall of the pit was a long yellow banner with blue lettering:

PEYTONA RACING

82

and a shorter purple one with yellow lettering proclaiming the name of the team's sponsor:

WABASH GUITARS

Inside the rectangular pit box in front of those banners were three long tables set end to end and covered with yellow and blue cloths.

Grandpa Hotshoe was still talking. "After an

hour and a half," he said, "at about eight o'clock, the general public is let in. There's an hour or so for them to get autographs and souvenirs, or buy stuff and eat. Then, at about nine, the eating and autographing end, and the dancing begins."

Kin glanced at the Peytona pit. There were only a few people gathered in front of the blue-and yellow draped table. Cope was there with his wife and kids. He was talking to a couple of crew members from other teams.

There was no sign of Waddy. Or either of his children. For a second, Kin felt disappointed.

Then he caught himself. *Don't be stupid,* he told himself. *She'll be here soon enough—you'll have plenty of time to make a big fool of yourself. Meanwhile, maybe . . .*

"Grandpa," he said, "could we walk out on the track? Would NASCAR mind?" It was something he'd wanted to do since first coming to the race track this summer.

Hotshoe smiled at him understandingly. "Not at all," he said. "In fact, in a little while they'll be opening the gate by the flagstand to let people in."

They walked across the grassy strip toward the track. The closer they got to the asphalt, the faster

Kin's heart beat. They stepped onto the pavement, and all of a sudden Kin became aware that they were walking uphill.

He peered down the straightaway toward turn one. "Whoa!" he said. "It's not really a straight-away. It makes a gradual, sweeping bend down toward the turn. And it's so—so steep! I thought it was flat."

"It's steep all right," Hotshoe said. "But wait till we get to Daytona—and Talladega and Bristol. Then I'll show you some really steep banks. We'll go down between turn one and two, and it'll be so steep you won't be able to walk up it. If the track's hot and a little gritty, you'll slide right off."

Kin looked down the tilted-left straightaway, into the still more steeply banked turn, and tried to imagine what it would look like at 150 mph, with cars on both sides of you, in front and in back. . . .

"Awesome," he said with a low whistle. "Driving a race car must really be incredible."

Hotshoe chuckled and put a hand on Kin's shoulder. "It's the only thing in the world more fun than digging fishing worms. Now, come on. Waddy should be here by now. Let's go back and say hello to your teammates."

As they left the track and started back across the grassy strip, Kin saw that more than a dozen people had arrived at Waddy's area since they'd left. Men, women, and children were milling around in front of the blue-and-yellow draped table. He recognized a portly figure in a white suit as Hollis Wabash, the team's sponsor. Waddy himself was sitting at the table nearby, chatting with a driver from another team. Several other people were already seated near Waddy, though Kin couldn't see them from where he was. Was Teresa among them?

Hotshoe was glancing around. "I wonder if your brother and sister are around here somewhere."

"They're probably spending all their money at the taco stand," Kin said, feeling a little distracted. "You know how Laptop loves hot sauce."

"You're probably right," Hotshoe said. "Well, except for the part about the money. Everything here is free to us racing people, and most folks know Laptop and Laura are with me."

"Free?" Kin said. "Cool!" He glanced at the fast-food stands with more interest. But he could also see plenty of coolers and picnic baskets stacked behind the table in the Peytona area. He had a feeling he wasn't going to go hungry tonight.

"Come on," Grandpa Hotshoe said again. "Let's get over there. Waddy's waving at us."

RUNNING OUT OF TIME

The light coming through the narrow truck windows was fading and turning pink as the sun set. Laptop had fallen asleep and was snoring softly. Laura's stomach was grumbling hungrily. She hadn't eaten much lunch—for one thing, she'd been too busy helping Annie. Also, she'd figured she would get plenty to eat at the dance.

I wonder if it's started yet, she thought, absently picking at her fingernails in the dim light. *I wonder if my dorky brother will manage to ask Teresa to dance? I wonder if Laptop and I . . .*

She gulped and stopped the thought before she could finish it. She sat up and glanced around, once again looking for a way out. But there was none. The truck's rear door was shut tight and locked from the outside, and the windows were too small for them to fit through even if they could have reached them.

She sighed as the roar of the tractor reached a higher pitch outside. How long would the crazy twins keep looking? What would they do if they never found anything? She didn't want to think about the possibilities.

Laptop was still sound asleep. For a moment, Laura considered waking him, just to have some company. But she decided against it.

Let him sleep, she told herself. *No sense both of us sitting here being terrified. . . .*

RULE NUMBER THREE

Kin was only a few steps from the Peytona team table when he spotted her. She was sitting between Waddy and Junior in the middle of the long table.

"Teresa!" he said before he could stop himself.

She looked up and saw him. Her face broke into a dazzling smile. "Hey, Kin!" She waved. "Come on and sit with us."

Kin gulped and took a step forward. Teresa looked more beautiful than he'd ever seen her. Her honey-blond hair, usually gathered in a casual ponytail, spilled loose over her shoulders. Her violet eyes sparkled, set off by the cornflower-blue dress she was wearing in place of her usual jeans or shorts.

"Hey there, Hotshoe," a woman's voice called out from farther down the table. "Who's this handsome young fellow you're hanging out with these days?"

Kin turned to see who had spoken. A woman was smiling at him from the seat beside Waddy. Her eyes were green and her blond hair was cut short, but there was no mistaking the resemblance in her face. She could only be Teresa's mother. Teresa looked as much like her as Junior looked like his father.

"Uh, hi, I mean, hello, Mrs. Peytona." Kin stuck out his hand, feeling a bit awkward. He had known that Teresa and Junior had a mother, but he'd never really thought much about her. When he'd met the other Peytonas at the track in Tennessee, Mrs. Peytona had been off visiting relatives for the week. Suddenly aware that everyone was watching him—including Teresa—he stammered out, "I'm Ki—uh, McKinley, uh, I work for—that is, Grandpa Hotshoe—"

"I know who you are, Kin," the woman replied with an easy smile, taking his hand with a firm grip. "The kids can't stop talking about you, and neither can Waddy. So glad you could come!"

"Uh . . ." Kin wasn't sure what to say. His eyes wandered toward Teresa again.

- - - - - - - - - - - - - - - - -

"As you can see, the boy's glad to be here, Helen," Hotshoe said with a chuckle. "So am I. Thanks for letting me hang around."

Kin was sure his face was bright red. As Teresa turned away to listen to something her father was saying and Hotshoe walked over to greet Hollis Wabash, he quickly scooted into the empty seat beside Junior.

"Hey, man." Junior grinned. "This is cool, isn't it?" He waved a hand to indicate the entire scene.

Kin nodded. He noticed a piece of orange paper on the table in front of him. "What's this?" he asked, picking it up.

Teresa heard him and leaned forward from her brother's other side. "It's the rules," she said. "They're put on every table and passed out to fans when they come in."

Kin scanned the piece of paper. It read:

CHECKER FLAGG'S RULES

FOR

THE PIT ROAD SCRAMBLE

(THE SEABREEZE EAT, MEET, AND

DANCE-TO-A-BEAT FROLIC)

1. NO AUTOGRAPHS AFTER THE MUSIC STARTS.
2. NO DANCING AFTER THE MUSIC STOPS.
3. NO WATERMELON ON PIT ROAD AFTER MIDNIGHT, JUNE 4, 1995.

"Has your granddad told you the story behind rule number three?" Junior asked Kin.

Kin shook his head.

"Hey, Daddy!" Junior called down the table to Waddy. "Kin hasn't heard about rule number three!"

Waddy leaned forward. "Really?" He called Hotshoe over. "I can't believe you never told the boy about rule number three," he said accusingly.

Hotshoe groaned and rolled his eyes. "I don't want to tell that story again," he said.

Hollis Wabash had followed Hotshoe over to the table. "If there's a story to be heard, Mr. Hunter, I'd sure love to hear it," he said in his deep, booming voice. He hooked his thumbs into his lizard-skin belt. "So you'd better just start talking."

Hotshoe grinned. "All right," he said. "If you insist." He cleared his throat. "That rule was established several years ago, just after the 1995 Pit

Road Scramble. The race and the scramble had been growing in popularity, and Checker Flagg, the owner of Seabreeze Raceway, wanted to do something to show his appreciation to the fans. When he heard that watermelon was cheap because of a bumper crop down in Florida, he bought a truckload. And he advertised that year's event as the 'Fan Appreciation Scramble—Free Watermelon!' People just flocked in.

"Checker had pickup trucks all up and down pit road, their beds filled with ice and watermelon. Soon after the infield and grandstand gates opened, the tables were full of people eatin' away at watermelon. Even though the night was hot enough to make a jaybird sweat, a lot of fans were wearing their race jackets to show which driver or make of car or brand of oil was their favorite. Well, at one point a fan wearing a Jeremy Mayfield jacket noticed a guy at the next table, his back turned, goin' at his watermelon like a buzz saw. This guy had on an old Cale Yarborough T-shirt and bib overalls that kinda stood out at the side—sort of like a trick-or-treat bag asking for something to be dropped in it."

Hotshoe chuckled.

"Well, you can imagine the rest. The Mayfield man talked his little boy into sneaking over there and dropping a chunk of ice-cold watermelon down this fellow's overalls. It took a few seconds before the cold feeling hit, and when Mr. Bib Overalls turned to see who'd done it, a young woman wearing a Jeff Gordon T-shirt walked by, holding hands with a guy who had Dale Earnhardt's name and number painted on his bald head. Wanting to take revenge and figuring they'd done it, Bib Overalls decides to attack the boyfriend.

"Since he'd already eaten almost all of his watermelon, Bib Overalls said, 'Excuse me,' and reached across the table and grabbed a piece of watermelon off the plate of a guy in a Darrell Waltrip hat. Well, the Waltrip fan didn't like having his food grabbed off his plate like that. He jumped up and ran after Bib Overalls. And before you could say Ricky Rudd, there was an all-out watermelon fight goin' on all up and down pit road. Rusty Wallace fans gathered in bunches to ward off attacks from Dale Jarrett fans, who kept running away from Intimidator fans until they decided to join forces with the Bobby Labonte and Terry Labonte fans and storm the pickup truck where the Rainbow Warriors had set up their defenses."

Hotshoe shook his head, his eyes twinkling like twin stars as hoots and chuckles came from his audience. Kin just grinned and listened, prouder than ever to be Hotshoe's grandson.

"The beginning of the end came," Hotshoe went on, "when a bearded man stuck a 'Mark Martin for President' flag in the pile of ice and watermelon in one of the pickups, then backed it down pit road, going faster and faster as people scattered to get out of his way. He slammed on the brakes, and the flag and the whole load of ice and watermelon went sliding out the back and onto the asphalt, with watermelons rolling and bouncing and splattering everywhere. Well, by then, the Rusty Wallace and Ernie Irvan fans had caught on to the idea, and soon all the ice and watermelon that had been in the back of pickup trucks was a big watermelon slush on pit road, with all the fans out there together, young and old, eating and splashing and having a fine old time. Checker Flagg said it cost him more to clean up the mess than he made selling tickets for the race."

When Hotshoe had finished, Mrs. Peytona leaned over and winked at Kin. "And that, Mr. Catch-can Man, is why we have rule number three."

EATING AND AUTOGRAPHING

"Come on," Junior said after Hotshoe's story was over. He hopped out of his chair and punched Kin on the shoulder. "Let's go check out the booths."

Kin glanced down the table. "Uh, won't we be eating soon?" He didn't want to admit it to Junior, but he was more interested in staying there and talking to Teresa than wandering around with her twin brother.

Teresa glanced over at them. "Mama hasn't even started unpacking the food yet," she told Kin, pushing back her chair. "We've got plenty of time to look around before it's time to eat."

"We?" Junior pretended to be annoyed. "Who invited you to come with us?"

"Kin did," Teresa said playfully, taking Kin's arm. "Didn't you, Kin?"

"Uh . . ." Kin couldn't seem to make his voice work right when she was standing that close. Luckily, neither she nor Junior seemed to notice. The two of them were already squabbling good-naturedly as the trio moved off toward the row of food booths.

Before long Kin relaxed a little and started having fun. He and Teresa and Junior made their way down pit road, sampling the fast-food fare at every booth they came to.

They weren't alone. The track was alive with people of all ages, including a lot of kids around their age. Almost all the kids wore racing team T-shirts, hats, or jackets. What struck Kin most was that nobody seemed to think of themselves as special. Wasn't everybody's dad a driver or engine builder or tire changer or dump-can man?

Before Kin knew it, it was almost eight o'clock. "We'd better lay rubber," Teresa said, glancing at her watch. "Daddy said to be back at the table by eight for the autograph session."

Junior nodded. "Daddy says it's rude if fans come in and we're out wandering around like we don't care."

When the gates opened promptly at eight, Kin and his friends were back in their seats with the others, sampling Mrs. Peytona's delicious fried chicken and coleslaw as they waited for the fans to pour in. Kin noticed that the first fans to hit pit road were boys—most of them around ten or twelve years old. They all carried autograph books and ran like crazy from table to table to get as many autographs as they could.

The first ones to the Peytona table came running up breathlessly. "Please sign, Mr. Peytona!" they cried, slapping their books down in front of Waddy. As soon as he'd signed, they were off again, looking for another driver.

But after the first flurry of driver-crazy boys, Kin found the fans to be remarkably polite and patient. People talking to Waddy were mindful of those behind them. After talking for a minute or two, they'd step aside and let someone else up. No one seemed to mind if others crowded around and listened, either to their question or Waddy's answer.

Cope, Tach, and Carl were occasionally asked for autographs by the more knowledgeable fans, who also had interesting questions about race strategy, engines, or suspensions.

Some fans wanted to get autographs from everyone—including Kin. He felt self-conscious the first

few times he signed his name on a T-shirt or autograph book, but the fans who asked were so nice
that he soon started to relax.

Kin was signing an autograph book for a kid
from Missouri when a short, round-cheeked girl
with a mass of dark, curly hair approached him.
Behind her was a boy with sand-brown hair. They
both looked about Laura's age. "Hi," the girl greeted
Kin cheerfully as the Missouri fan thanked Kin and
moved off. "Do you know Laura Travis?"

"She's my sister," Kin said. "I think she's around
here someplace if you're looking for her."

The boy was staring at Grandpa Hotshoe, who
was sitting beside Kin. "Wow," he said. "Can I
please have your autograph, sir?"

"Sure thing, son." Hotshoe reached for the
piece of paper the boy held out.

The girl wasn't paying attention to them. "Are
you sure she's around?" she asked Kin, her round
face looking slightly worried. "Have you seen her
yourself lately? Or Laptop?"

"No." Suddenly Kin felt his stomach clench nervously. When had he last seen his brother and sister?
He couldn't quite remember. Laura had definitely
been at Annie's at lunchtime, but after that . . . For

a second, the image of those nutty clone kidnappers flashed through his mind. Laptop had a way of finding trouble when you left him alone too long. "Why? Is something wrong?"

"I'm not sure." The girl played nervously with a strand of her curly hair. "When I got home a little while ago, there was this weird message on my answering machine. It got cut off, but it was from Laptop and Laura . . . "

Kin didn't wait for her to finish. He was already out of his seat, glancing worriedly at his grandfather. Luckily, Hotshoe had turned away to greet another fan, and he hadn't heard a word. That was good—Kin didn't want to worry him unless he had to.

"Come on," he told the two younger kids urgently. "Let's go."

"This is a disaster." Zo kicked at the rusted-out body of what must have once been a large two-tone station wagon. "How could you idiot kids actually think this hunk of junk was treasure?"

"How could you be stupid enough to believe a seven-year-old boy had actually found a buried treasure?" Laura shot back hotly.

"Hey!" Laptop protested.

But Laura didn't pay any attention to him—or to Bo's and Zo's menacing glares. She was past the point of being scared by now. The twins had just dragged them out of the truck to show them what all their digging had finally turned up. An old wreck of a car. That was what the metal detector had found. If the situation wasn't so horrible, she would have laughed.

Bo ran his flashlight beam over the rusty wreck once again. It was well after eight o'clock and the summer sky was almost dark. The chirping of crickets and frogs was growing louder with every passing minute. But the twins didn't seem to notice any of that. They were too angry.

"This whole caper was a mistake," Bo spat out. "It was supposed to get us in good with the Big Boss, after the last fiasco when we lost all those cars we'd stolen. Now the Big Boss is going to be madder than ever."

Zo nodded. She glanced at the kids. "Well, maybe it won't be a total loss," she said, that evil glitter returning to her gray eyes. "At least killing these two will be fun."

"Good evening, race fans! Is everybody ready to par-tay?"

The voice came booming over the PA system, so loud that Kin winced. He was hurrying toward the race track's back gate, following the two younger kids, who had hurriedly introduced themselves as Jane and Eddie. For a moment, he wished he could be back at pit road, getting ready to "par-tay" with the others. But he couldn't turn back—not when his little brother and sister might be in trouble. They could be pains in the neck sometimes, but they were family.

"Have no fear, DJ Christ-o-pher is here," the voice on the PA continued, sounding a bit quieter as Kin and his companions found themselves standing outside the race track grounds, just behind the main part of the grandstand. "I'll be spinnin' everything from golden oldies to the latest hip jive for your listenin' and dancin' pleasure. . . ."

FAMILY REUNION

"I can't believe those two got themselves into trouble again," Kin muttered, as he followed Jane and Eddie across the wide, open field behind the grandstand.

Jane glanced at him over her shoulder. "We're not sure they're in trouble," she reminded him. "It's just a possibility."

"A strong possibility," Kin said with a sigh. He shook his head. Some people had normal brothers and sisters—Junior and Teresa, for example. Neither of them had to spend half their time worrying about what the other might be up to. "How'd I get so lucky?" he muttered sarcastically under his breath.

"What'd you say?" This time Eddie turned to look at him.

"I was just wondering how much farther it is to the spot where they think they found this treasure," Kin said. He wished he'd thought to bring a flashlight—it was pretty dark out here, even with a thin moon casting its faint, silvery glow over the scene.

Jane pointed to a spot ahead of them, near a patch of woods. "I think it's that way. Over where those—*eep!*" she squeaked.

"Check it out!" Eddie gasped. "Lights! They are over there!"

Kin looked where they were pointing. Several hundred yards away, a couple of pinpricks of light were bobbing up and down. It was too dark to see much, but Kin guessed that the lights were flashlights. "Thank goodness," he muttered. "Come on, let's go get them. I've got a few words to say to them. . . ." He jogged off toward the bobbing lights with Jane and Eddie right behind him.

He squinted as he ran, trying to see what his wacky brother and sister were up to. But the figures with the flashlights were in the shadows of the forest's edge, and it was hard to make them out. The lights kept disappearing behind trees and rocks, especially one huge boulder . . . or was it a boulder? Kin squinted harder. It looked kind of big . . . and square . . .

He was only fifty yards away, still peering ahead, when his foot struck something hard, almost tripping him.

"What the—" He paused, stooping to retrieve the object from the grass.

Eddie and Jane stopped, too. "What is it?" Jane panted.

Kin gulped, staring in confusion at the familiar box he was holding. "It's Laptop's computer," he said slowly. His heart started pounding. "He never lets this thing out of his sight. That must mean—"

"Worf!"

The familiar bark brought Kin up short. "Scuffs!" he exclaimed, and the little dog leaped into his arms, almost knocking the computer to the ground again. "What are you doing here? And what happened to you?" The dog was covered with burrs and brambles and dirt, as if he'd been hiding in the woods.

"Worf! Worf!"

"Hey!" a man's voice shouted from just ahead. "Sounds like that annoying little mutt is back."

Kin gasped and clamped a hand over Scuffs's

muzzle to keep him from barking again. The voice had come from the direction of those lights!

"That. . . that didn't sound like Laura or Laptop," Eddie whispered.

"Way to state the obvious," Jane whispered back sarcastically.

"Shh!" Kin hissed. He crouched down in the long grass. "I think we should find someplace to hide."

But it was too late. One of the flashlight beams turned and started bobbing toward them. "I'll go take care of the little beast once and for all!" a female voice exclaimed loudly.

"Uh-oh. She's coming right toward us," Jane murmured, her voice shaking. She and Eddie were huddled down beside Kin. In the near-darkness, Kin could barely make out their frightened faces. "And she sounds mean!"

"We'd better run for it," Eddie suggested.

Kin was about to agree. Whatever was going on here, he couldn't see Laura or Laptop anywhere. The best thing would be to go back to the track and tell someone about these people.

But before he could make a move, Scuffs wriggled free. Letting out a sharp "Worf!" he sprang out of Kin's arms and hit the ground running. "Worf! Worf!" he yapped loudly.

"Scuffs!" Kin hissed. "Come back here!"

The little dog paid no attention. He was already racing off into the darkness. The only way Kin could follow his movements was by the rapidly fading barks.

"He's heading off to the right!" the woman's voice cried from ahead. "Come on, help me get him!"

"Let's go!" the man growled loudly. "If he keeps barking that way, someone's bound to hear him sooner or later."

Both flashlights headed off after Scuffs. "I think that's our cue to leave," Jane said.

Kin wasn't so sure. Now that the bright flashlights were disappearing in the distance, he could see that strange boulder a little better—only it wasn't a boulder at all. It was a van. What was a van doing parked way out here at this time of night? Where were Laura and Laptop? And exactly who were those two people anyway? They had sounded a little familiar. . . . "Just a second," Kin said, suddenly suspicious. "I want to check something out first."

He handed Laptop's computer to Eddie and jogged toward the van, being as quiet as he could. There was no telling when the people with the flashlights would be back.

Jane and Eddie tagged along as Kin crept closer to the van. Soon they were only fifteen feet away, so they could see that the sides were unmarked. "Are you sure this is a good idea?" Jane whispered anxiously.

"Yeah." Eddie glanced over his shoulder toward the flashlight beams, which were still visible in the distance. "We really ought to—*aaah!*" His comment ended with a startled shout as he tripped over a rock and sprawled facefirst in the grass.

Kin winced. "Uh-oh," he muttered.

"Hey!" A shout came from the direction of the flashlights. "Is somebody there?"

The adults had heard Eddie's cry!

"Let's get out of—wait!" Kin had already turned to run, but then he heard something. Something coming from the van. A pounding noise, and— could it be? He listened more intently.

"Help!" a faint, familiar voice cried.

Then another. "Hey! We're in here!"

"It's Laura and Laptop!" he exclaimed.

"Those people are coming!" Jane cried, her voice panicky. "They'll catch us all!"

"We've got to get them out!" Kin didn't bother to waste any more time arguing. He didn't care what the other two did—he wasn't going to leave his brother and sister there.

He sprinted the remaining distance to the van, heading directly for the back doors. He saw immediately that they were wedged shut tightly with a thick wooden bar. "Hold on!" he shouted, grabbing the bar. "I'll get you out!"

"Kin?" Laura shrieked from just inside, her voice muffled by the door between them. "Kin? Is that you?"

"Hey!" The angry shouts were already much closer. "Who's there? What are you doing?"

Kin gritted his teeth and yanked harder at the bar. It wouldn't budge. His hand slipped and he felt a splinter dig into his palm, but he didn't stop. "Aargh!" he exclaimed. "This thing is really—"

"Move over," Eddie said, as he and Jane appeared at Kin's side. They still looked terrified, but they each grabbed a section of the bar.

Kin didn't have time to do more than shoot them a grateful look. "Okay, on three," he said. "One, two . . . "

With grunts and groans of effort, all three of them pulled at the bar at the same time. This time it worked. The bar flew up, and a second later Kin had the doors open.

"Come on!" he cried, spying Laura and Laptop's pale faces in the van's dim interior. "We've got to—"

"Not so fast," an evil voice commanded from just behind him.

Kin turned slowly. A flashlight beam snapped on, nearly blinding him. Shading his eyes, he squinted at the two people standing there—and gasped. That sleek, silvery hair, those glittering silver-gray eyes . . .

"It's that pair from before," Laptop's voice explained from behind him. "They're not really clones, just twins."

"But they're really nuts," Laura added.

"Silence!" The man waved his hand, and something glinted in the flashlight's beam. A gun!

Kin gulped. They were really in trouble. "Uh-oh," he muttered aloud. "What do we do now?"

The woman heard him and grinned. "Now," she replied, "you die!"

Suddenly Scuffs appeared. "Worf!" The little dog flung himself between the kids and the twins, then went straight for the man, leaping at his face.

The man was startled. "Wha—" He threw up his arms to protect himself. The gun went off, blasting into the air. "Aaah!" the man exclaimed, losing his grip on the backfire. The gun flew off into the darkness.

"Are you all right?" the woman exclaimed. Her flashlight wobbled crazily as she hurried toward the man.

Kin knew this could be their only chance. "Run!" he cried, grabbing Laptop by the hand and dragging him out of the van. "Run for your lives!"

The next few minutes seemed to last a lifetime. Kin raced across the field toward the comforting but impossibly distant lights of the grandstand. He never loosened his grip on Laptop's hand, half-dragging the little boy along with him. Nearby, he heard the others' feet pounding along on the grass.

There were shouts of anger from behind them, and a few "worfs" from Scuffs. "Are they following us?" Laura panted, as she raced along beside Kin.

Kin didn't have the breath to answer. He just kept running. A moment later they all heard the distant roar of a van starting.

Were they going to come after them in the van?

Kin put on another burst of speed, his heart pounding away like a jackhammer in his chest. "Hammer down," he murmured, remembering the familiar racing term for going full speed.

Suddenly Laptop stumbled and almost fell. "Wait," the little boy wheezed. "Slow down. I can't run anymore."

Kin shot a desperate glance at the grandstand, still a good distance away. But he had no choice but to slow the pace. "Wait," he said, realizing something. "The van. It's moving away from us!"

It was true. The sound of the motor was growing fainter every second. "They must have given up," Eddie panted. "They're trying to escape."

"Worf! Worf!" At that moment, they heard Scuffs racing toward them, barking all the time.

"Here, boy!" Laptop exclaimed, collapsing onto the ground as the little dog leaped onto his lap and started licking his face. "Good dog. You saved us!"

"You sure did." Laura bent down to pat Scuffs.

Kin rested his hands on his knees, trying to get his breath back. He glanced over at Jane and Eddie, then down at his brother and sister again. They were safe! "How did you two end up out there, anyway?" he asked.

Laura rolled her eyes and jerked a thumb at Laptop. "It was all his idea. Naturally."

Laptop shrugged, still panting. "I guess it was. But you see, it was like this . . . "

The next few minutes were busy with explanations. As the five of them—and Scuffs—walked slowly on toward the grandstand, Laura and Laptop both talked at once, so fast that Kin had trouble keeping up with it all. Jane and Eddie looked even more confused than he felt. But eventually it all started to make some sense.

". . . so then they threw us back in the van," Laura explained. "After they'd found that rusty old car and realized there was no treasure, they'd decided to k-kill us."

Laptop nodded solemnly. "But first they needed some time to dump all the dirt back in the hole they dug."

Laura shrugged. "In addition to being loony birds in general, they're neat-freaks, too."

"Right." Laptop nodded again. "By the way, thanks for coming to rescue us. I'm glad we're safe." Just then he spotted his Apricot 07, which was still tucked under Eddie's arm. He reached for it with a cry of joy. "All of us are safe!"

Before long, Kin and the others had returned to the race track, tracked down Grandpa Hotshoe, and dispatched the police to go and search for the evil twins. Kin was slightly tempted to go out there and help—but only slightly. The police could do the job on their own. And he was much more interested in getting back to the dance before it was all over.

As Grandpa Hotshoe bombarded Laura and Laptop with worried questions, Kin slipped away and headed toward the Peytona pit. Waddy and Cope and several others were standing in a group, laughing loudly, probably trading racing stories. Nearby, Junior was leaning against the table, talking to a cute girl with short hair and blue eyes. But Teresa was nowhere in sight.

"There you are, Kin," Mrs. Peytona said, looking up from a conversation with Cope's wife. "Where did you run off to?"

"Uh, nowhere," Kin said, glancing around for Teresa. Where was she?

As if on cue, she arrived at that moment from the direction of the dance floor, breathless and pink-cheeked. "Kin!" she cried in surprise, as the DJ announced the start of another fast-paced rock'n'roll song. "Where'd you go before?"

Before Kin could answer, Waddy detached himself from the group of men, raised one hand, and said, "Okay, team. Anybody wants to dance, do it now. There's a race tomorrow, and we need to turn in early."

"Oh, Daddy!" Teresa said. "The dancing's practically just started. Why do we have to be the first ones to leave?"

"We're not the first. Mark Martin and his crew left thirty minutes ago."

Teresa frowned. "Well, maybe Mark Martin just doesn't like to dance."

"Not likely," Waddy said with a smile. "You know Mark's a physical fitness nut. If a man in his kind of shape needs a good night's rest, so do I."

"Come on, Daddy," Teresa pleaded. "At least let us stay for one more slow song."

"Yeah, Daddy," Junior added. "Kin just got back from wherever he ran off to. You've got to let him get in at least one slow dance before we go."

Waddy opened his mouth—to say no, Kin was sure—but Mrs. Peytona leaned over and whispered something in his ear. He looked first at Kin, then at Teresa. "All right," he said. "One slow dance. Then we hit the road."

"Thanks, Daddy." Teresa jumped up and gave Waddy a hug. She gave Kin a sidelong glance, then turned to Junior and the blue-eyed girl. "Come on. Let's all go out there and dance while we wait for that slow song!"

The DJ played three or four more fast songs before he finally announced a slow dance. Kin had been dancing as part of a group that had started out as four people, then swelled to six and then eight and ten and more, until Kin had completely lost count. In the end he'd found himself in a crush of dancing teens, feeling lucky if he caught a glimpse of Teresa every few minutes in the crowd.

As the first notes poured out of the loudspeakers, Junior came over and nudged Kin in the ribs. "Step to it, buddy. This is your last chance."

Kin glanced at him quickly. "What do you mean?"

Junior grinned. "Don't think I haven't noticed the way you've been mooning after my sister," he said. "Personally, I don't know what you see in her—she's ornery, she's stubborn, and she thinks she knows everything about everything." He shrugged. "But hey—to each his own."

For a second, Kin felt embarrassed. Were his feelings really that obvious? But he shrugged it off as Junior hurried off in the direction of the cute blue-eyed girl.

Suddenly Kin noticed that Teresa was looking at him from several yards away. He swallowed hard. The moment of truth was at hand.

Just as he started toward her, a tall, tanned, athletic-looking boy of about eighteen walked up to her. He took her hand and led her to an empty spot on the crowded dance floor.

Kin's throat tightened. His face turned red. "Who's that?" he asked Tach, who happened to be walking by at the moment, hand in hand with his wife.

Tach paused and glanced over at Teresa and her partner. "That's Elt—short for Eliot—Bethea. Young stud driver from California. Started in go-karts and midgets. Kind of a Jeff Gordon story. Already won a couple of Grand National races."

"They say he'll have a NASCAR Winston Cup ride in a couple of years," Tach's wife chimed in. She was a comfortable-looking woman with kind brown eyes. "May even try for rookie of the year next year."

Tach nodded. "That's right. But hey, kid, no big deal. Go out there and cut in. That's one reason they call it a scramble. Anybody can cut in."

"Really?" Kin glanced over at Teresa. She was smiling at something Elt Bethea had just said, looking more beautiful than ever. "I don't know. I'm not sure I could do that."

Tach looked at him sharply. "Well, then maybe it's just as well," he said. "I've known Teresa since she was a little girl, and she likes her fellows bold. Driver types. Aggressive. Always cutting for the lead. I guess that's not you, is it, Kin?"

"That's harsh, man," Kin said, glaring at the engine man in surprise.

"It was meant to be," Tach said, swinging his wife into his arms and starting to dance. "Now, get out there and make your move, or forget about it!"

"Excuse me, may I cut in?"

Elt Bethea frowned and stepped away from Teresa.

Teresa smiled and took Kin's hand. Kin nervously put his arm around her waist. *How close should I hold her?* he wondered. *Is Mrs. Peytona watching? Is Waddy?*

Teresa leaned back and smiled at him, her hand resting lightly in his. "I was beginning to think we weren't going to get to dance together," she said. "When you disappeared like that earlier . . . "

"I . . . I was thinking that, too," Kin said. "That Elt guy—do you know him?"

"A little." Teresa smiled again, her voice playful and teasing. "Why do you ask?"

"Oh, no reason. Just wondering."

At that moment, Kin saw a girl walking toward them, weaving her way gracefully through the other dancing couples. She was very pretty, with black hair and dark eyes. Though she was small, she moved with confidence.

The girl made a beeline for Kin and Teresa. *Just my luck*, Kin thought in annoyance, pulling Teresa a little closer. *I finally get up my nerve to dance with Teresa, and some girl wants to talk to her!*

But instead of talking to Teresa, the strange girl asked, "May I cut in?"

Teresa looked as angry as Elt had looked a moment before. "If you say so," she said, tossing her head.

The newcomer moved smoothly to take her place. Before Kin knew it, one of her slender hands was wrapped in his own while the other rested on the back of his neck. They started to dance, the girl seeming to anticipate Kin's every step before he took it.

"Uh, hello," Kin said, feeling decidedly awkward at this turn of events. Awkward and confused. "My name is McKinley Travis, but people—"

"People call you Kin," the girl interrupted. "I know."

"You do?"

"I've seen you around the track."

"You have? So what's your name?" Kin asked.

"Someday."

"Someday's your name?"

"Someday I'll tell you," the dark-eyed girl said with a smile. The music stopped and she stepped back. "See you around," she said, and quickly disappeared into the crowd.

Did that really happen? Dazed, Kin shook his head and walked toward the Peytona table. Hotshoe was the only person sitting there.

"Teresa wasn't feeling well, so they all left," Hotshoe said. "They all said to tell you good-night.

Waddy also said for you to get to bed pronto." He stood up. "By the way, the police haven't found those two lunatics yet." He frowned and shook his head. "But anyway, I already sent Laura and Laptop home. They're exhausted, poor kids."

"So am I," Kin said, suddenly much less interested in staying at the scramble now that Teresa had left. He yawned. "I guess it's been a long day for all of us. Let's go."

RACE-DAY MORNING

Kin was leaning forward over the RV's small dinette table so he wouldn't drop anything on his blue-and-yellow race-day uniform. He was eating the last of the bacon and eggs Hotshoe had made for him. Hotshoe had finished breakfast and was putting his dishes in the sink when they heard a knock.

"Must be Annie," Hotshoe said. "Who else would it be at this hour?"

He opened the RV's metal door. "Adrian!"

Kin looked up in surprise. He'd almost forgotten that Aunt Adrian was supposed to return to North Carolina that day. He glanced at his watch. To come all the way from South Carolina by that hour, she must have started driving before the crack of dawn. "Hi, Aunt Adrian," he said. "Want some breakfast?"

Laptop sat up in his bunk, yawning and squinting at the doorway. "Aunt Adrian?" he said sleepily.

"Hello, McKinley. Good morning, Larry." Aunt Adrian smiled at Kin and Laptop, then stepped aside and gestured at her long, black car, which was parked nearby. "The man out there by the limo talking to Henri is my friend Jim Sheridan. I was surprised to learn that he's a NASCAR fan. I told him about you, Hotshoe, and he wanted to come down here as early as possible. He thought maybe you could get him into the pits."

"The pits. Sure, but . . ." Hotshoe frowned and glanced worriedly at Kin and Laptop. "First I have something I need to tell you. It's about Laura and Laptop."

"Laura and Laptop?" Aunt Adrian said. "What do you mean?"

"It's nothing, Grandpa," Laptop said quickly, sounding much more awake now. He swung his feet over the side of his bunk and gave his aunt a wide, innocent smile.

Kin glanced at his little brother sympathetically. He was probably in for some major scolding once Aunt Adrian heard what he and Laura had done the day before. *Of course, she probably won't be too happy with me, either,* he thought. *She'll probably think I should have been helping to keep an eye on them.* He sighed. Sometimes it wasn't easy being the oldest.

"You see, Adrian," Grandpa Hotshoe began, looking decidedly uncomfortable, "it seems that yesterday, while Kin here was busy with his work and I was busy with mine, Laura and Laptop were getting themselves involved in quite an adventure. I realize it was my responsibility to look after them while they're here, and I couldn't feel guiltier about the whole thing, especially considering how much worse it all could have been, but—"

Aunt Adrian was looking more and more confused with each word. She turned to Kin. "What on earth is he talking about?"

Kin gulped. "You see, Aunt Adrian," he said, "it's like this. . . ."

Twenty minutes later, the whole story had come out. Laura had been called over from Annie's trailer, and Aunt Adrian's friend Jim Sheridan and her chauffeur Henri had wandered over from the limo. The whole group was gathered under the awning joining Grandpa Hotshoe's RV and Annie's Airstream. Scuffs was sitting quietly at Laptop's feet.

Aunt Adrian was fanning herself with her slim leather handbag, even though the morning was still cool. "I can't believe it," she murmured. "I simply can't believe it." She stared at Laura. "Larry is just a child. But you—how could you go along with this, Laura?"

Laptop answered for his sister. "We thought it would help pay the ransom for the painting Smedley stole," he explained.

"No one has proven Smedley stole anything!" objected Aunt Adrian. Suddenly she gasped. "Wait a minute. How did you know about that?"

Kin gulped, suddenly realizing that he had played a bigger part in this escapade than he'd realized. "Um, I guess that's sort of my fault, Aunt Adrian," he admitted. "I, uh, was worried when you showed up here the other day acting so weird. So I followed you when you were talking to Grandpa, and overheard the whole story." He glanced at his brother. "Oh, and Laptop tagged along, too."

Aunt Adrian gasped, looking shocked. But her

friend Jim Sheridan, a tall man with short gray hair, chuckled. "Very enterprising, McKinley," he said. "With gumption like that, I may have to try to lure you away from the race track to work for my company someday."

Kin grinned at the man, liking him immediately. "Call me Kin," he said.

"This is terrible!" Aunt Adrian said, fanning harder than ever. "You could have been killed. And all because of me."

"Well, all because of Uncle Smedley, actually," Laptop corrected. Laura kicked him in the shin.

"Burried treazzure!" Henri exclaimed in his thick French accent, looking down his long, thin nose at the kids. "Did you actually belieeeeve . . . "

"Enough, Henri," Aunt Adrian said sharply. She sighed. "What's done is done. The kids were just trying to help."

"It was a noble attempt. I don't know if anything can help us now, though." Jim Sheridan gave Aunt Adrian a comforting pat on the arm. "That ransom is due by tomorrow, and I just don't think I can scrape enough money together by then." He frowned. "Besides, I don't like the idea of paying off those rotten thieves." He glanced at Aunt

Adrian again. "No offense to your Smedley, of course."

Kin bit back a grin. He suspected that Jim Sheridan didn't think much of Smedley, either. Suddenly he realized they'd all been talking for a while. "Yow!" he cried, glancing at his watch. "I've got to go. I'm going to be late for work." He hesitated, glancing at Aunt Adrian. She still seemed kind of upset about what had happened. Would she still let the kids stay with Grandpa after all that? "Um, I mean if you—"

"Go ahead, McKinley," Aunt Adrian interrupted with a small smile. "Hotshoe told me how much this job means to you. And I realize it's the day of the big race—Jim talked my ear off about it the whole drive up here this morning."

Jim Sheridan grinned and winked at Kin. "Guilty as charged," he said. "Good luck today, Kin."

"Thanks!" With that, Kin took off at a run in the direction of the garage gate.

Laura was feeling worse and worse. Kin had left an hour ago, Grandpa Hotshoe still wore the hangdog look he'd had since hearing what they'd

----

been up to, and Aunt Adrian was fanning away with her little handbag as if her life depended on it. The three of them were sitting on some folding lawn chairs beneath Grandpa and Annie's awning, along with Laptop and Scuffs. Jim Sheridan had left to track down some business associates, and Henri was over by Aunt Adrian's limo.

Meanwhile, the seconds and minutes were ticking away. Laura seemed to be the only one who remembered that she had a job to do today, too. She had promised to sing the national anthem before the start of today's racing, and she had planned to do some practicing this morning.

"Aunt Adrian," she began, "I know you're upset, but I really have to—"

"Upset?" Aunt Adrian interrupted. "Upset? I don't think I've been this upset since I found that ransom demand from Smedley." She sighed and shook her head sadly. "Laura, I thought you were the sensible one. McKinley has always been a bit of a dreamer, and Larry, well . . ." She let her voice trail off.

"Larry, well, what?" Laptop demanded, sounding insulted.

Aunt Adrian reached over and patted his hand,

which was resting on the case of his Apricot 07. "It's just that you're still very young, dear," she said soothingly. "You count on your big brother and sister to help you."

Laptop snorted, but he didn't say anything. He just rolled his eyes at Scuffs, who was sitting beside his chair.

Laura didn't know how much more time had passed before Aunt Adrian finally seemed a bit calmer. Laura herself wasn't feeling calm at all by that time. Jim Sheridan had returned, and he and Grandpa Hotshoe had wandered off in the direction of the pits. Meanwhile, Laura and Laptop were still sitting by the RV with Aunt Adrian, who seemed unwilling to let the two kids out of her sight.

"Maybe we should go over and get ready to watch the race soon, Aunt Adrian," Laptop suggested tentatively at last.

Laura glanced around. The area nearby was almost empty. Everyone had left to get a good seat to watch the day's racing. She gritted her teeth anxiously. "Like I've been trying to tell you, Aunt Adrian," she said. "I'm supposed to sing today, and I—"

"Yes, yes, dear," Aunt Adrian said distractedly. "That's nice. Now, tell me again where you got this metal detector you two used?"

Laura gritted her teeth, feeling ready to explode. She wasn't normally a very patient person, but she'd been trying hard all morning to keep her temper under control. Her aunt was already unhappy with her because of the treasure-hunting escapade, and besides, Aunt Adrian really hated raised voices. But at this point, Laura was feeling desperate. If she didn't start getting ready soon, there was no way she could get over to pit road in time to sing the national anthem and open the races. Maybe shouting was the only way to get that message across. She took a deep breath—

"Laura!" a new voice exclaimed. "What are you doing just sitting there, girl? You should be getting dressed for your big performance!"

Laura could hardly believe her eyes or ears. Annie! She was saved! The woman had just arrived, fresh from her restaurant. She hadn't even bothered to remove her apron, which was stained with the remnants of that morning's breakfast selections.

"What's that?" Aunt Adrian turned to stare at

Annie curiously. "A performance? Laura, are you supposed to perform at the race today?"

"Yes, Aunt Adrian," Laura said with as much patience as she could manage. "I'm supposed to sing the national anthem in just a few minutes."

"Well, for goodness sake!" Aunt Adrian exclaimed. "Why doesn't anyone tell me these things?"

Laptop was feeling a little disgruntled as he walked toward pit road with Aunt Adrian. Kin had escaped hours ago. So had Grandpa Hotshoe. Laura had just hurried off, breathless but looking great in a nice outfit, carrying her Wabash guitar.

And here he was, stuck with Aunt Adrian. She was treating him like a baby, insisting on holding his hand as they walked. She hadn't even let Scuffs come with them—he was back in the RV right now, all by himself. Laptop felt lucky that she hadn't made him leave his Apricot 07 there, too. She had given it a questioning look as he tucked it under his arm.

"I don't know, Larry," she was saying now. "Maybe you're too young for this sort of life. Maybe you ought to come back to Boston with me as soon as I get this Smedley thing worked out."

"I'm fine down here with Grandpa, Aunt Adrian," Laptop insisted for the fifteenth time. "I'm sure this sort of thing won't happen again."

"I wish I could be sure about that," Aunt Adrian said. "I really don't—"

"Hurry up, you two!" Grandpa Hotshoe's familiar voice rang out from just ahead.

Laptop looked up and spotted his grandfather and Jim Sheridan waving at them from the Peytona team's pit.

"Hurry, Adrian—your niece is about to perform," Jim Sheridan called.

"Come on, Aunt Adrian." Laptop tugged at his aunt's hand and moved forward impatiently. He didn't want to miss seeing Laura sing. As annoying as his older sister could be sometimes, she always sounded great when she performed.

"All right, all right." Aunt Adrian laughed. "I'm coming. I want to watch Laura as much as you—"

Suddenly she broke off with a loud gasp. Laptop glanced up at her face, which had gone dead white. She was staring at the pit they were passing.

Laptop looked over at the pit himself. All the

people in it were dressed in gray coveralls with none of the colorful patches or embroidery that most of the team uniforms sported. The car they were working on was all gray, too. A tall man wearing a driver's uniform was standing beside the car. Laptop squinted at the driver. He looked kind of familiar. . . .

Aunt Adrian was staring at the driver, too. She strode over to him, dragging Laptop along behind her. "Smedley!" she said to the driver accusingly. "What in the world are you doing here?"

More later . . .

About the Author

T. B. Calhoun is the pseudonym of an experienced mechanic who has written on automotive topics as well as penned award-winning science fiction and fantasy novels. Like Darrell Waltrip, Jeremy Mayfield, and other NASCAR stars, Calhoun is a native of Owensboro, Kentucky. He currently resides in New York City.

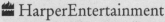